ROXIE N★BLE

AND THE FASHION FRENZY THIEF

*AN UNOFFICIAL
ROBLOX STORY*

BY JOY4104

ISBN: 978-1-947997-00-4

Cover Design by Sophia Jin

www.fiverr.com/efeidesigns

Chapter 1

My Life Wasn't Ruined After All

When you picture a secret agent, what do you see? A hero in disguise? Mom or Dad? (You know how they are, hiding thingama-bobs in super-duper top secret compart-ments where no one can find them...not even themselves.) Or maybe a snake wear-ing a miniature badge? More on that later.

I'm none of those...and definitely not a snake. My name is Roxie Noble. I am part of a secret agency in the Robloxian Universe and winner of the No-Mission-Completed prize. All I've done at the headquarters was train and hope that one day Agent Barnes would give me my own mission to accomplish besides feeding his pet snake. Yeah, I wasn't kidding about the snake with a badge thing.

I sighed, leaning on one hand while stroking Mr. S, the snake. I had to be at training in a few minutes, but I wanted to keep wallowing in my despair. Maybe Agent Barnes would see me and take pity. Perhaps I would have a little luck on my side.

"Roxie!" Agent Barnes yelled, slamming his hand on the door-frame to his office. "Stop spoiling my snake and get your butt to the meeting room!"

Meeting room? My stomach fluttered. "Yes, sir!" I said, trying not to laugh at his red, pinched face. I ran past him and down the hallway. Could this be the day? Would my dream come true? A spontaneous meeting could only mean there were new missions! I dashed forward, passing by other fellow agents conversing as they walked toward the meeting room.

Sliding to a stop just outside the door, I smoothed my hair and tried to look casual as I walked into the room in case any of the high-ranked agents made it here first, but looking around I saw no one. I grinned, skipping inside.

But wait. I wasn't alone after all. There, leaning against the back wall was Mr. Goody-Two-Shoes.

I halted, my grin sliding off my face like ice cream on a hot day.

He lifted his eyes to meet mine and smirked. "Wassup, Roxie. You look quite chipper skipping in here," he said.

"Good morning to you too, Chris," I muttered, rolling my eyes.

He coughed saying, "Agent Smith to you."

"If you won't call me agent, I won't call you agent."

"You haven't earned your agent name, whereas I have, so you should call me by my respectable title."

I didn't respond. Yeah, he was lucky enough to have completed his first mission not too long ago. My eyes landed on his first star pinned to his jacket and moved my hand up to where my own would be when I was considered an official agent. I felt my cheeks burn with embarrassment.

I had been at the Robloxian Secret Agency, or RSA, for years and had yet to be given a mission. Apparently, I was "too young" or "too naive" or "too vulnerable." They thought I wouldn't be able to keep a secret or that I'd be too weak to capture the enemy. Pfft. They were wrong. And I was gonna prove them wrong. Someday...

Sighing, I plopped down in one of the cushy meeting chairs and drummed my fingers across the long, wooden table. Agents started pouring in, joining me at the table until there were no seats left. Agent Barnes sat at the front of the table and cleared his throat before speaking.

"We have several missions to attend to." He listed off each one and who was going to work on it. I squeezed my eyes shut, hoping that my name was going to be called. Anytime now...

"...and that's all the missions I have for now. Good luck agents," Agent Barnes finished. I cracked my eyes open, then shoved my fists into them to keep from crying. Again nothing. I stayed frozen in my seat as agents rushed by anxious to get started on their objectives.

The door slammed closed and, thinking I was alone again, I started moaning, "Nothing. No mission for me yet. Uuuuugh. My life is an absolute wreck. I'm not important to anyone or anything!" I slammed my fists on the table, finally looking up, and froze. Agent Barnes cleared his throat, staring at me with raised brows. In his hands, he clutched the mission papers he had brought in. I blinked and he cleared his throat again.

After a few awkward, silent seconds, he said, "I see you covet those missions I handed out."

"I...what?" I asked, still coming out of misery thought-land and into the present.

"You really want one of their missions. You're jealous, hmm?"

"I guess…"

Agent Barnes sighed. "Don't think groaning means you'll get your way, but there is one, small mission that I didn't give to anyone." He frowned and held out the paper for me to see. "It didn't seem to need our attention. Just a simple thievery going on at Fashion Frenzy that the Robloxian police should be able to handle."

I grabbed the page from him and scanned the words, not believing my eyes. Fashion Frenzy was hosting their famous Robloxian Fashion Show Contest that anyone could participate in. The rules were simple: dress up for the theme of the fashion show and hope the other Robloxians voted for your style.

I looked back up at him, a grin spreading across my face. "This is my mission? My very own mission?"

He nodded slowly, squeezing his lips together in a thin line as if disapproving my excitement. I did have a tendency of acting overly dramatic...

"OH MY CRABCAKES! I HAVE MY OWN MISSION!" I started skipping around the meeting room, holding the paper in front of me.

"Pull yourself together!" Agent Barnes stopped me with his words and I stared at him, with my eyes opened wide at his demanding tone. "You have twelve hours to complete this. If you don't succeed, who knows how long it will be till I give you another mission. You start tomorrow morning. Take this time to prepare," he huffed and with that, he walked out of the meeting room, his face red again.

"No mission is too small for me," I whispered to myself, biting my lip to keep in a squeal of joy. After doing a little jig, waving the paper in my hand, I skipped out the door towards Pops' office.

I burst through the door without knocking. "Pops! Pops!" I yelled, waving the page at him. He looked up from his computer, a smile forming under his gray whiskers. "I got a mission!" I announced, beaming.

Pops wasn't actually my father, but he was like a father to everyone at RSA. Before being called Pops, he was Agent Hixon, but he stayed on after passing his duties to Agent Barnes. Pops was the oldest agent here and I liked him more than Agent Barnes. He had been mentoring me ever since I came here.

"Congratulations Roxie!" he said. I handed him the paper and he skimmed through it, flicking his eyes across the page. "So you have to find the thief who has been stealing clothes and accessories from Fashion Frenzy and turn them in. Are you preparing?"

"I wanted to tell you right away first," I gushed, bouncing on my toes. "I mean, I don't have to prepare that much. It's just a simple case of thievery."

"Nothing is too simple," Pops said, clasping his hands together on his desk. "Don't overlook the details. Don't assume."

"Oh, I won't, Pops."

"Good luck, Roxie," he said with twinkling eyes and a warm smile.

Chapter 2
Spring Dance Fail

Vivid colors of pink and orange and blue and white enveloped me and a fizzing sound like a soda can opening filled my ears while teleporting into Fashion Frenzy the next morning. After landing in the server, standing in the center of the lobby, I bounced on my toes and drummed my fingers on the side of my leg, wondering what I should do first. I skipped over to the spectators' window and watched the participants choose their outfits for the round's theme. I must've just missed joining in.

I had passed Chris ("Agent Smith") before being transported and couldn't hold in a wink and a proud grin. He rolled his eyes and stomped away. All I could think about was that he'd have to call me agent too if, no, *when* I completed my mission.

Excitement bubbled in my stomach. I would become an official agent. I would no longer be called newbie or any other insulting name.

I took in a deep breath. The round ended and Robloxians were back in the lobby waiting for the next contest to begin. Glancing around, I went through my mission's key factors. All I had to do was finish first in three games to be able to find the thief's secret hideout and figure out who was this thief. With RSA's tech, they figured out the server with the extra room, AKA the hideout, and knew the thief would be on the same server.

I could feel my particles being shifted from the lobby into the fashion room. My heart lurched, anticipating the competition. I was frozen where I stood as the other Robloxians were transported in and I had time to look around. Gasping at all the fabulous clothes, I itched to start.

Focus. I looked into the accessory room and noticed an empty hat stand as well as a pair of shoes missing. I needed to find this thief.

My heart jumped as the speakers crackled to life. "The theme is...Spring Dance!" Everyone unfroze and I zoomed towards the dress area with focus like a cheetah chasing its prey. And I prayed that I'd find the perfect outfit.

I scanned the different dresses as other girls shoved me, trying to get a good look as well. I planted my feet firmly to the ground. There was no way I was gonna lose because someone desperate pushed me away.

I ran my fingers across the different dresses. What would look good at a spring dance? A long, black, sparkly dress? No, too formal. How about a pink, leathery dress? The color said spring, but the leather said rain boots. I shook my head and looked through other dresses, unaware of the time ticking by as fast as it took for a spy to disarm a bomb.

As I neared the end of the dresses, my eyes landed on one. Pulling it out, I "oohed" at the pretty, pink, yellow, and blue flower designs contrasting against a white dress. This was the one!

I stepped away from the dresses and noticed I was the only one left. Gulping, I ran towards the accessories and saw girls and guys wearing their outfits. Only a few stragglers were left picking out accessories...and I was one of them. I glanced at the time and cried out, "What? Only thirty seconds left?"

Dashing towards the shoes, I saw blue ballet flats. I grabbed them and sprinted towards the changing rooms. There was no time to collect any extra accessories. I whimpered as I yanked my clothes off and threw on the dress and shoes. Maybe if I had time I could grab a purse or hat.

I opened the door and, just as I stepped out, my body froze. "Time is up!" the speaker said. I groaned.

I blew a loose strand of black hair out of my face after getting teleported into the waiting room before the fashion show began. I hadn't even had time to take my hair out of its ponytail and do something with it.

It was hard to work with such limited allotment of time.

Limited time...I glanced down at my watch. At least I still had eleven hours left for my mission. My chest loosened and I let out a breath. I could do this. I would prove to Agent Barnes that I was capable of being a secret agent. I stood up straighter and put on a confident smile.

"Roxie Noble!" the speaker shouted, announcing my entry to the runway as it teleported me. Digesting the butterflies in my stomach, I sauntered across the catwalk, beaming and waving. At the end of the runway, I stopped and struck a pose. There were cheers and lights flashing and I couldn't help but blow a kiss into the crowd. The attention was thrilling and made me feel alive. Like I was worth something. I wanted to feel this way as an agent and have people in RSA look up to me for a change.

I twirled around and started walking back, but as I neared the exit, my waving faltered. Tuning out the noises, I slowed my pace. Something had caught my vision. Were my eyes playing tricks on me? No. Only secret agent eyes would notice the ink in tiny scribbling on the wall.

I know you're here, secret agent. You won't find me. —T

Chapter 3
A New Friend And A New Fiend

I didn't win that fashion show. I didn't even place, but I felt wonderful. I had tried to suppress my happiness, but giggles would burst through my lips.

Even though that note sounded threatening, and a small part of me was nervous, I was so glad to know the thief was actually here and RSA's tech hadn't glitched, as it had before. One time an agent had gone to a beach server following clues and he sent back scrambled letters for us to unscramble. When Agent Barnes typed the letters into the computer, the words it produced were, "You Go Cheer." After an hour of the agent cheering on the beach with nothing happening, Agent Barnes figured out the computer used totally different letters. Agent Barnes and the computer's reputation plummeted for a few weeks after that incident.

I walked into the bathroom, typing on my watch to call Pops. Every Robloxian was given a watch after going through the process of being accepted into the agency and it looked like a high-tech watch that only a rich person would wear. On this one, though, you could call, set timers, write notes, and anything else a secret agent would need. It even had a voice recorder!

After knocking on every stall door to make sure I was alone, I clicked the dial button on Pops' number and waited for him to pick up. Being a secret agent meant you had to be, well...secretive.

"Roxie! How are you doing on your mission?" Pops said, after answering my call.

"Hi Pops!" I answered, then proceeded to tell him all the events that had happened including the message on the wall. "So it was signed with 'T' and that must mean it was from the thief!"

I could hear him mumbling nonsense, then he spoke up saying, "Roxie, you have to be careful. They know you are here. It doesn't sound like they know who you are, but that means you have to be stealthier."

"So I have to be sneaky about being sneaky and not look like I'm trying to be sneaky?"

"Exactly," he said. "Keep your eyes open for anything or anyone out of the ordinary. Don't rush ahead either. Make sure you have all the facts before telling us who you think the thief is. Call back if you need more help. Good luck!" He ended the call and I sighed. I knew I had to keep a lookout and get all the facts. I did go through basic training.

The bathroom door was pushed open and I looked up from my watch and walked towards the sink, acting like I was just finishing my business.

A girl with orange hair walked past, then looked back at me. "Hey, you were the one without accessories right?" she asked in a chipper voice.

"Um, yeah," I said twisting the faucet on. It sprayed everywhere. "Ugh!" I cried, jumping back. Great. I quickly turned off the water and started wiping my shirt with paper towels.

The girl chuckled, saying, "You had good style, but you need to bedazzle it up a bit next round! I'm Kat...with a 'K,' though I do love cats."

Kat loved cats. I made a mental note. "Nice to meet you. I'm Roxie." We shook hands and something clicked. "Hey, aren't you the girl who won this last round?"

She grinned and nodded. "I play this game so much; I win almost every round! It's so fun!"

"Wow," I said, not really sure what to say to that. "Well, I gotta go!"

"See you later!" Kat said, and I walked out of the bathroom.

So Kat loved cats and also loved this game, and was obviously good at it...I was going to have a hard time winning three games in a row.

I sighed and wandered around the lobby. I eyed the other competitors. There were several girls and boys. Hmm…If I was going to be a thief what would I look like?

I'd probably wear expensive clothes. Most of the Robloxians here did wear fancier clothes though, so I couldn't strike out any for sure non-thieves. The best thing to do would be to actually talk to them.

"Hi!" I said, waving to a blonde girl sitting by herself.

Her head shot up and she shoved her black, studded cellphone into her matching handbag. "Hi," she replied, eyeing me as if I'd been spying on her. Which technically was true; I was supposed to be spying on everyone.

"I'm Roxie," I said, holding out my hand.

"Sarah," she replied, shaking my hand without a cordial smile. Then she proceeded to get up and walk away.

Frowning, I watched her leave. What a snob. No way was I going to be talking to her again anytime soon.

"Don't worry about her," a voice said behind me. It was Kat again. She stopped next to me and continued, "She's always like that. Come on, I'll introduce you to some of my friends." She strutted off and I followed her like a helpless, lost kitten.

Chapter 4
Is A Red Scarf That Important?

I was introduced to a few of Kat's friends who were in the same server, but she said she had lots more. I couldn't even remember their names except for Rebecca who had blue hair. I smiled and nodded as Kat and her friends continued talking about the latest fashion trends.

"Roxie?" Kat asked, and her three friends looked at me as if expecting the answer to why the earth wasn't cubed. And honestly, why couldn't it be? Weren't we all block people here?

I hadn't been paying attention and they were still looking at me. "Yeah, what, huh?" I said, placing a hand on my burning cheeks, red with embarrassment. Rebecca snickered.

Kat placed a hand on her hip and sighed. "What brought you here to play Fashion Frenzy?"

"Oh, you know," I said, waving my hands, "fashion stuff is fun. Who doesn't like clothes?" Phew, that was close. Why did I feel like I was being interrogated?

Before the next question, the speakers came to life announcing the next round, and we were all teleported into the clothing area. Everything on my mind dissipated. My heartbeat drummed in my chest. I anticipated the race. The competition. Adrenaline raced through my veins and I bit my lip. There was no way I would run out of time this round. I would be victorious.

The speakers crackled again. "This round's theme is...Fall Festival!"

I scanned the newly spawned clothes. Everything was in red, orange, yellow, gold, and brown hues and as soon as I unfroze, I zipped over to the clothes and grabbed the first outfit that caught my eye. No time to waste!

Next, I ran toward the accessory area, scooting past other running competitors, with clothes hanging over my shoulder. Sarah the Snob, Kat, and Rebecca were there already. Kat's usual friendly face was set in a focused scowl as she moved through the hats with efficient swipes of her hands. I came up beside her and looked through the hats myself. I noticed an empty spot.

"Did someone pick up this hat?" I asked Kat, while deciding whether or not to pick an orange top hat or a headband of leaves.

"It was gone when I got here," Kat said, shrugging, not stopping her swift work.

I made a mental note, then moved on from the hats choosing the headband. I picked up the rest of my accessories and was headed to the changing rooms when I heard shouting.

"Let go! I wanted this first!"

"No, I picked it first fair and square!"

I looked back at the accessory room and saw Kat and Rebecca playing tug-of-war with a red scarf. I couldn't just leave them fighting!

I bundled up my clothing and left it by the dressing rooms. I ran to where the fight was happening and grabbed on to the scarf as well. Both girls quieted and turned their glaring faces at me.

"If you aren't careful," I said, firmly, yet quietly as to not cause more attention, "you are going to rip this scarf. What would be the good in that?"

"This was going to complete my outfit and she took it from me!" Rebecca said with tears in her eyes.

"No, I had it first!" Kat argued.

I checked the time and, rushing through my words, said, "Look, there are only two minutes left on the clock. Aren't there other scarves or accessories one of you can use?"

"I want this one!" Rebecca whined.

"Becca, please! There's no time!" Kat said, clutching the scarf.

"You guys are friends! You should be able to handle this kindly," I said, then held my breath, wondering what would come about in these tense seconds.

Rebecca lowered her eyes and huffed, "Fine, you can have it. I'll get something better." She threw her end of the scarf at Kat and stomped away.

"Thanks for helping, Roxie! You're a good friend," Kat said, giving me a hug. "I'm sure Rebecca and I will still be friends. She nice, just sometimes...well..." She waved her arms in the air acknowledging what just happened.

"Ah, I see," I replied with an awkward laugh, then continued saying, "We better change before the time runs out!" I ran back to where I left my clothes.

In the waiting room, after the clothing round finished, I sat on a purple beanbag, waiting for my turn to walk the runway. My black, shimmery skirt was bunched up near my knees clad in orange leggings.

I studied the Robloxians around me. Maybe the thief was that guy in the top hat...or maybe that girl in the plaid blouse. Thief, thief, thief...who are you?

An idea sprang on me and I sat up straight. The thief wouldn't want to be caught, right? So they would try to fit in. And stealing for so long without being caught meant they would have had to play for a while. They would be good at this game.

I hated to think my new friend, Kat, could be the thief, but I added her to my mental list of suspects. I added Rebecca too. Both of them were fighting over that scarf as if it were a life or death problem. Maybe that scarf was super expensive? Then I added one more name. Sarah. I hadn't seen her a lot, but I didn't like her...maybe she was the thief.

"Roxie!" Kat called.

"Over here," I replied and waved my hand till she saw me. She raced over, an expression of concern and anger on her face.

"I cannot find my scarf! I think Rebecca stole it from me, but she says she didn't."

I perked up at the word "stole." Rebecca stomped over.

"I told you I didn't steal it! You lost it yourself!" Rebecca fumed.

"Girls, what—" I was cut off as the speakers announced my name and teleported me to the catwalk.

They'd have to deal with their argument by themselves this time.

I started my walk, but all I could think about was that red scarf. Specifically, who stole it. Rebecca could be lying, or maybe Kat was setting her up to make it look like she was the thief? Or maybe it was someone else entirely.

Chapter 5
A Truth Or Dare Interrogation

Back in the waiting room, I was anticipating who had won the round. I squeezed my eyes shut and hoped with all my might it was me. I needed this win.

While strutting across the runway, the crowd had cheered for me. I saw cameras flashing and colorful lights focused on me. I made sure to add a cute twirl at the end.

Then I looked for a scribbled note like from the first round, but there was nothing.

I sighed. To find the thief, the first question I would ask suspects was how long had they been in here. Only the thief would stay in this server for a very long time. Interrogating the players here wouldn't be a bad idea. I couldn't call it that though. What would get people to spill secrets...?

Truth or Dare.

I smiled as my subterfuge came together. The watch beeped and I glanced at it. Six hours left! Half the day was gone already!

The speakers crackled to life saying, "And the results are in!" Everyone was teleported to seats near the winner podiums enclosed by a rope fence. My heart fluttered and my fingers drummed my leg to the beat of the background music.

"In third place...Rebecca!" Everyone clapped as she walked onto her podium. "In second place...Kat!" I bit my lip. I had to win first...I just had to! "And in first place...Roxie!" I screamed and pumped the air. Everyone probably thought I was crazy. I ducked under the rope and skipped up onto my podium, waving at the crowd. I looked down at Kat, hoping she'd share in my joy, but all I saw was disappointment.

We were teleported back into the lobby to wait for the next round and I met up with Kat.

"I can't believe I won! I'm so happy!" I gushed, not able to contain my excitement.

"Yeah, good job," Kat said with a half-hearted smile.

My own smile faltered. "Why are you so disappointed with second? That's still good!"

Kat huffed and crossed her arms. "I would've won if it wasn't for Rebecca. My red scarf was missing from my outfit!"

I frowned. "It's not like they would've handed you the victory just because of a red scarf."

"I know; you're right," she sighed. "Even if it truly wasn't Rebecca who took my scarf, I'm upset someone would actually steal."

"I know. Crazy, huh," I said. Kat didn't know there was actual thievery going on. I spoke up, "I say we play a game with everyone to lighten the mood. How about Truth or Dare?"

"Yes! I love that game!"

Soon we had a big circle made with several players including Rebecca. Kat dragged Sarah in, too, even though she didn't want to play.

I started first. "Rebecca, truth or dare?"

"Truth," she said after a second. I smiled. Just what I wanted.

"How long have you been playing this game?"

"Aw, that's a boring question," Kat said.

"Hey, it's her question and I will answer it fairly," Rebecca said, obviously thankful she didn't have to answer anything embarrassing. "I've been playing for a couple of days now and on different servers."

A couple of days and on different servers. I didn't think Rebecca would be the thief then. Already this game was working to my advantage!

The game went around a few times before someone chose me.

"Dare," I answered, not wanting to risk spilling anything about my agent life. I was the first person to do a dare.

"You need to do a front flip, then a back flip," Sarah said with a raised eyebrow.

Gasps came up from the circle. Kat spoke up again, "That's a bit much, don't you think? We're at the runway, not a gymnasium."

But they didn't know I had training that consisted of learning these simple flips. I stood up, took a breath, and performed the two flips, landing on my feet both times. I looked up with a proud smile. I saw shocked faces and a few people nodded at me, impressed.

"Shall we continue?" I asked, plopping back down.

I wasn't able to cross Kat or Sarah off my list of suspects after we ended the game, but at least Rebecca was off. I was hoping

Kat would be taken off the list, but I still wasn't sure...

I walked into the bathroom, the only place where I could be alone to think, and began pacing, my shoes echoing off the tiled floor. "Who could it be..." I mumbled, forgetting to check if anyone was there to hear me.

A crash sounded from inside a stall and I jumped.

"I'm okay!" Kat said, stumbling out with a half-zipped backpack over one shoulder. She blew a stray red hair from her face, looking flustered.

"What are you doing in here?" I exclaimed, my heart still slowing from the scare.

"What are you doing in here?" she asked back.

"Obviously we're both not doing what a bathroom is used for," I said, crossing my arms. "But seriously, what was that noise?"

"Um…" she blinked, stammering," um…you know…"

I narrowed my eyes, suspicion crawling over me. "No, I don't know…"

She blinked and sniffed. Then her whole face turned red and fat tears started rolling down her cheeks. "I'm sorry. I didn't want to do this…but after I started I couldn't stop!" She blubbered, covering her face with her hands.

My heart clenched. Was she about to tell me she was the thief all along? My friend…a thief? I didn't want to believe it.

"I…I…I wanted to stop a long time ago, but I couldn't. I wanted the fame and the money, so I could buy better clothes and be popular and maybe even be an inspiration.

But it was wrong, I know," Kat continued, wiping her nose on her sleeve.

"It's okay," I said, sure that I had found the thief. "You've admitted you were wrong and now I can help you stop taking what's not yours. You need to come with me though."

"O-okay, away from this game?"

"Yeah, for now. We need to talk about what you've done."

"Like a therapist?"

"Um...sure." I shrugged. "Now follow me." I walked out of the bathroom and shook my head, not believing I had uncovered the truth so suddenly. And that it had been Kat all along.

Chapter 6
The Worst Part Of Being An Agent

Blinking against the fading colors after fizzing into existence at the RSA, I grabbed Kat's wrist and started pulling her towards Agent Barnes' office. In the midst of everything, I'd forgotten to handcuff her. We passed several agents who stopped what they were doing to watch me, the agent noob, with my first caught culprit.

"What? Where are we? Why do the people look so serious and have badges and everything?" Kat whimpered, jerking her head all around as she took in her surroundings.

"Why do you think? They, I mean, we are the real deal," I said, entering Agent Barnes' office, forcing on a proud smile. It was bittersweet taking Kat in. She was my friend, but she was also a thief. She lied to me! And I was going to be promoted for completing this job. All I had to do next was win two more rounds to find the secret room.

I shoved open the door and dragged Kat up next to me. "Agent Barnes, I brought in the thief," I announced as he raised his eyes from his computer.

"Thief?" Kat exclaimed, looking at me with wide eyes and a slacked jaw.

"What did I say about coming in without knocking?" Agent Barnes said at the same time.

"I thought we were going to a therapist not a police station," Kat whispered forcefully.

"This isn't a police station," I scoffed, placing my hand on my hip. "We are secret agents!"

"I'm not a thief!" Kat wailed, throwing her hands into the air.

"That's what all criminals say. Anyway, we'll find out with the truth detector."

"Are you sure she is the thief, Roxie?" Agent Barnes squinted at me as if trying to find a problem. I bristled at his lack of confidence in me. He was the one who gave me this mission!

"Yes, Agent Barnes, I am sure of my capabilities. And, yes, this is the thief."

"Roxie, I don't understand!" Kat cried out, putting a hand to her head. I ignored her, but the feeling of betraying my friend pierced my heart. No, she betrayed me first. This was my job...my duty.

"Roxie, find the secret room. We'll report our findings on this suspect," Agent Barnes said, waving her out.

I fled from the room, not able to endure his impertinence or Kat's tear-stained, frightened face.

Chapter 7
My Life Might Actually Be Ruined

Even though I was back in the same Fashion Frenzy server, there were hardly any of the same players left. Only Sarah and Rebecca remained from when I was there last.

"Hi," I said, as Rebecca came up to me.

"Hey, where's Kat? I wanted to make sure we were back on good terms. She's usually always on and she just left suddenly without warning."

I guess she didn't know I had left at the same time. Good. I didn't need anyone getting suspicious that I was a secret agent. I shrugged in response, not feeling up to talking.

"Oh...okay," Rebecca said, shrugging as well, and just as we were teleporting into the clothing area, she said, "Good luck at the next round!"

"You too," I said, trying to refocus my thoughts on my mission. Only two more wins needed since, thankfully, I made it back in time for my previous win to count.

"The theme for this round is...Pop Star!" the speakers boomed.

I didn't have the same adrenaline or motivation as I'd felt before. Not when my friend turned out to be an actual thief. I had to do my duty as an agent, though, and I couldn't fail.

I chose my outfit and changed into it. I didn't smile as I looked at the pop star in the mirror wearing tall boots and a glistening, turquoise dress. I didn't even feel excited that I won the round, but I at least smiled for the cameras and thanked Rebecca when she congratulated me.

I sighed and sank into a huge, pink beanbag in the waiting room. As an agent it was hard to have true friends. You had to lie about your identity, and investigate, and apparently sometimes accuse your own friends.

Rebecca walked over to me and crossed her arms. "Look, I've noticed that you haven't been yourself this round and you don't have to tell me why or whatever, but seriously, stop moping." She plopped down next to me.

"What am I supposed to do after something terrible then?" I said, crossing my own arms.

"Obviously not mope," she said again, rolling her eyes. She huffed and continued her rant, "Eat chocolate, play a game, do something that makes you happy. All you're doing is making yourself feel worse and, in turn, making people stay away from you. Good golly, that fake smile you put on after winning definitely lowered the mood here."

"Sorry," I mumbled. She had no idea what I was going through, but at least she tried to help even if she was a bit brash. My watch dinged, alerting me of a message.

Call me. —Agent Barnes

"I'll be back," I said to Rebecca and dashed into the bathroom. I checked all the stalls again this time, then dialed his number, hoping for the best.

"Bad news, Roxie," Agent Barnes said before I could even say "hello." I rubbed my arm, suddenly feeling cold.

"What is it, Agent Barnes?" I whispered.

"You are wrong about the thief." I could hear an edge of enjoyment in his voice as if he was glad I had messed up. Perhaps I should be glad too, if it meant my friend wasn't the thief after all!

"What do you mean?"

"This Kat is not the thief. She did have a way of cheating the game system so she could choose the themes, but that is her only wrongdoing in this server."

I held in a squeal and said, "I guess I was too fast to assume."

"You were, and as a punishment, I am lowering the time limit. If you don't figure out who the thief is in one hour, you will fail this mission and someone more adequate for the job will take over."

"What?" I yelped, my joy diminishing.

"Also, we are going to have to remove any of Ms. Kat's knowledge of us before she is free. Time is ticking, Roxie," he said, then hung up.

I dropped my arms and took in a shaky breath. On the bright side my friend was still gonna be my friend and not a thief, but now I only had one hour left to complete my mission and the next round wasn't going to start till several minutes later.

I did the only thing I could think of. Taking Rebecca's advice, I bought a huge cookie and started devouring it like a rabbit would with a carrot.

I only had forty-five minutes to complete my mission when the next round started. I raced through the clothes, picking out an outfit for the theme, "Fairy Tale."

Inside the dressing room, I adjusted my green, sparkly wings and attached a pom-pom to each of my green ballet flats. I scooped up my hair into a bun and added a sparkly tiara for extra glam. I could hear the time ticking away in the back of my head and I couldn't quite catch my breath.

Pacing the waiting room, I kept checking my watch. Thirty minutes...twenty-five...twenty... I could hear cheers from the audience fawning over my competitors' out-fits. I bit my lip and clasped my hands to-gether, trying to stop shaking. I had to win. I had to.

It was my turn to walk the runway and I made sure to perform a sassy wand twirl and pretend to fly off like the fairy I dressed up to be. The audience cheered for me too. I couldn't tell if they were louder and more exuberant than when the other competitors walked though. My head felt light and my hands shook.

Now I waited for the results with sixteen minutes to go. If I didn't win and unlock the secret room this round, I was going to run out of time before the next round even began. I chewed my fingers and bounced on my feet.

What would happen if I didn't complete my mission? I would be punished somehow. Would I never obtain my agent title? How would I ever be able to prove myself again?

We started teleporting to the podium room and I was startled out of my thoughts. Fear and anticipation raced through my veins. I had to remind myself to breathe.

"Are you excited to see who wins or are you still mopey?" Rebecca asked, walking over to me.

"Anxious," I replied, wringing my hands together.

She chuckled and said, "It's just a game."

For you it is, I thought.

The speakers shrilled, "Third place goes to...Jake!" A guy in a wolf outfit stood on the lowest podium, bowing.

"I really hope I get first this round. I feel like I did great on my outfit!" Rebecca beamed, swishing her red cloak around her.

"You did good on your outfit," I said, gulping down my panic. I needed to win.

"Second place goes to..."

Please, please don't say my name yet. I bit the inside of my cheek.

"Roxie!" the speakers finished.

I heard the cheers and congratulations from Rebecca and the crowd, but my mind was on my mission. I tried to plaster on a smile, but it felt more like a grimace. Second? I needed first! How was I…what was I going to do? My whole life was going to be ruined because of my failed mission!

"Roxie?"

I glanced up from my podium and saw Rebecca. I didn't even hear her name called out for winning first and I felt guilty.

"Congratulations!" I said, trying to sound excited.

Rebecca rolled her eyes and huffed, "Thanks. You're being a great friend right now."

My fake smile lowered into a frown and I looked down, clasping my hands together. "I'm sorry, Becca. I was just really wanting to win this round. I am glad it's you who won instead though."

"You know, I know I'm not as popular as Fashionista Kat, but I still want to be your friend," Rebecca said, crossing her arms.

"No, it's not that!" I said, feeling tears of frustration rising to my eyes. I swallowed the lump in my throat. I couldn't lose another friend because of my duty. I had to tell her. I opened my mouth to speak, but something caught my eye. I glanced over to where the figure moved and saw a blonde gliding through the walls as if she were a ghost. "Whaaa…?" was the only thing that came out of my mouth.

"Are you okay?" Rebecca said, raising an eyebrow.

"Someone just moved through the walls!" I said, pointing to where I saw the person.

"Um, that's illegal...hacking isn't allowed," Rebecca said, concern written on her face.

We were teleported out of the podium area and Rebecca and I met up at the bean-bags.

"I saw a girl—blonde hair—pass through the walls. No kidding!" I said, stumbling over my words.

"That's weird. Who would do that?" Rebecca said, crossing her arms.

"We should see who all has blonde hair here and find the suspects."

"Sarah," Rebecca said suddenly.

"Yeah, she does have blonde hair."

"But not only have I seen her acting snobbish and unsocial, I haven't seen any other blonde girls here for the past round."

I gasped and excitement bubbled up in me. What if this was connected to the thief?

Perhaps I wasn't going to fail my mission. "You would make a good secret agent, Becca!" I raved, then slapped a hand over my mouth.

"Thanks!" she beamed. "Wait...are you...?"

"Um..." I wanted to tell her anyway, but was I betraying the RSA? Too late.

"No way!" Rebecca exclaimed. She started laughing. "I knew there was something up with you! You were acting all strange and everything! And doing those flips at our truth and dare game? That was amazing and now I know where you learned that!"

"Yeah..." I said, letting out a relieved giggle. She wasn't mad at me for keeping it a secret. "But you have to keep it a secret!" I rushed on.

"I gotcha back, girl...now that I understand you," she said in a lower voice, grinning.

"So, friends again?"

"Um, I didn't know we weren't friends." Rebecca flipped her hair over her shoulder.

I smiled, but I still felt guilty about going against the RSA's rules and telling her. Right now, though, there was something more important at stake. "Let's go find Sarah."

Chapter 8
I Had Known It All Along

We spent the next few minutes searching the lobby for Sarah, but couldn't find her.

"She's still in the server, right?" I asked Rebecca, nervously rubbing my arm. I hadn't told her about my mission or the time limit I had, but I only had eight minutes left.

"Yeah..." Rebecca said, puzzled.

My watch beeped and I glanced at it. Agent Barnes wanted to speak to me again.

I sighed and told Rebecca, "I'll be back." I rushed to the bathroom and called him. "Hello, Agent Barnes."

"Roxie, you don't have much time left," he replied.

Of course you're gonna call just to remind me of my imminent doom, I thought. "I know. I'm working on it," I said instead.

"Well, thank your lucky stars that we have found the hidden room. It popped up on our screens not five minutes ago."

"What? Really?" I asked, my hand coming up to my mouth in shock. "I didn't win all three games in a row, though!"

"The secret door had been activated by someone else, then." The thief!

"Where is it?" I asked, excitedly.

"We will guide you."

We ended the call and I raced back to Rebecca. I needed her help.

"Rebecca!" I gasped, stopping my run.

Rebecca whirled around, alarm written across her face. "What? What is it?"

"I need your help," I said, rushing through my words. "Can you keep a lookout for Sarah and keep her in the server if she tries to leave?"

"Yeah, sure. Is something wrong?" She lowered her voice and said, "Is this part of a secret mission?"

"Yeah, maybe. Don't know for sure if she is the culprit, but it's looking that way," I said, still not wanting to reveal too much for RSA's sake. My watch beeped and I looked down. "I need to go. Thanks for helping me out!"

I ran towards the entryway to the audience room. An agent had texted me to go through here; they had unlocked the door already. I grabbed the handle, glanced over my shoulder, then opened the door. I let out a breath and snuck in.

I scanned around the darkened room, only a few dim lights hanging across the walls. It was weird being in the audience section instead of on the runway. And it was creepily empty and silent. Goose bumps rose on my arms.

Beep.

I jumped, then sighed, looking at my watch and reading the next set of instructions. Dropping my arm, I scanned around the room, looking for the flickering light. There. Since the thief had just used it, they found the door's location. They had to open it after I did my part since I didn't have the secret code.

I ran towards the light, barely different than the others. Every few seconds it flickered. I stopped under the light and looked up at it, squinting. Placing my hand on the wall under the lamp, I waited for something to happen. Nothing did. I read my instructions again and—oh. I moved my hand and touched the lamp instead.

Still nothing.

Wait.

The room started to shake, but ceased after a couple seconds. A number pad appeared.

I held my breath, waiting for the agent hackers to do their part in opening the door. The wall opened inward. I grinned and walked into the dark hallway. I followed the path, receiving no other instruction, one hand on the rough wall next to me.

My nerves started jumping and I felt shaky just like the room was a few moments before. I closed my eyes and inhaled. Opening my eyes, I took the next few steps. Light filled the next bend I took and I saw the exit.

I bit my lip and continued the trek, shielding my eyes with one hand until they adjusted to the light. I clasped my hand over my mouth at what I saw. A figure stood with their back facing me and was clothed in all black, including the hood over their head. But the whole room took my breath away. It was like stepping into the clothing area of Fashion Frenzy. Beautiful clothes were laid out everywhere and accessories and shoes on every shelf across the walls. I tiptoed into the room, getting out my new taser, just in case the thief did anything.

"Freeze," I said, but it came out as a squeak. I coughed. The figure whirled around and her hood fell off, blonde hair tumbling down. Sarah. I stifled my gasp. So it was the snob all along.

"I knew it," she muttered. Then, with more bravado, she said, "Roxie, don't do anything stupid."

"I won't," I said, my voice also getting stronger. "Why have you been stealing from this game?"

"I needed to," Sarah said. She paced in front of me, making sure to keep her distance and continued, "You wouldn't understand. You were privileged enough to be an agent from the start where I had to work up to where I am now."

I tilted my head. "You think I didn't have to work up to where I am now? And trust me, I'm not that high ranked or popular or anything." I kicked at the floor and looked down. "I've been waiting for this mission for a while now. I had to work and work and work every day for the past several years."

Sarah stopped pacing and stared at me. She hesitated before saying, "I guess we aren't so different after all…When I first joined, I was a noob with terrible clothes and nothing unique about me." She shrugged and continued, "I was bullied, so I decided to do something about it. I started robbing places and now I'm rich and I have cool clothes and people surround me when I have all my expensive gear on. I feel like a queen!"

"We aren't different when it comes to wanting to be a someone in the Robloxian Universe, but we are different when it comes to pursuing that. I didn't steal to get popular and I'm still not popular. I'm working on getting myself better for myself, not for other people," I said, feeling sorry for this girl.

"I was bullied! I had to do something to stop it and this worked." She crossed her arms, getting defensive.

"To be honest, I get ridiculed everyday. I let it motivate me, though, even if it does get under my skin. I also have a great person who helps me through it." I smiled, remembering Pops. He would be proud of me.

Sarah groaned, shaking her head. "I have to get away. You're gonna turn me into the police! My life will be ruined." She started walking backwards and opened a secret hatch, eyeing me warily.

I held out my hands and was about to shout, but then thought of something better to say. "Will you try to stop justice from happening or will you let this motivate you to do better when you're free?"

Sarah stopped and squeezed her lips together. After a couple seconds of silence, she drooped her head and sighed. "I want to do better..." she whispered. Sarah looked back up at me. "Take me in."

I smiled. "You're already doing better."

Chapter 9
Agent Life

Agent Barnes raised an eyebrow at me. "Are you sure she is the thief? You aren't assuming things this time, are you?"

We were in his office, Sarah standing next to me in handcuffs as protocol for criminals. I pursed my lips and held back a sigh. "Yes, sir. I'm sure she is the thief."

"I am…" Sarah confirmed, lips quivering. She looked down, hiding the shame written across her face. I patted her shoulder for reassurance. She did the right thing.

Agent Barnes' mouth quirked up into a half-smile. "You finally did something right…with some help from us. Good job, Roxie."

I gave him a curt nod, biting my cheek to keep from saying something I would regret.

"Well," Agent Barnes started, getting up from his desk, "I can take her off your hands. You are free to go."

I blinked. When would I get promoted? Was I going to stay a desolate noob all my life? I knew better than to ask. I backed up towards the door, but before I left, a thought occurred to me. "Where's Kat?" I asked.

"That suspect you brought in?" He sighed. "She's recovering from our procedure. If you want to talk to her, all she thinks is that she was extremely hurt playing Fashion Frenzy."

"Does she...remember me?"

He shrugged. "Who knows? We had to erase all her memory about her knowledge of the RSA. You were the one who led her to this," he said, not forgetting to point that out.

I turned around and ran from his office, not needing to hear more. I bit my lip. Kat just had to remember me! We were friends! It was all my fault if she didn't remember me. Maybe I deserved it. I skidded around a corner and down the stairs into the small rooms where they kept injured agents. I found out which room she was in from a kind nurse and quietly opened the door.

Orange hair caught my eyes and I knew I was in the right room. I tiptoed over to her bedside and saw her sleeping. Should I poke her awake? Should I leave her alone? I wanted to talk to my friend so bad and make sure everything was all right!

I scanned the small, sterile room and made a face. Honestly, someone should make these rooms a little happier with brightly painted walls and pictures and fun bed covers and pillows.

"Hello?"

I whipped my head back to Kat and found her staring at me, confused. "Hi, Kat!" I exclaimed, grinning.

"Um…" She looked around, then back at me.

My grin faltered. "Do you not remember me?"

Kat shrugged. "Not...really. Maybe..." She scrunched up her face as if trying to recall something. I squeezed my hands together anxiously. "Aren't you the new girl who was trying out Fashion Frenzy for the first time?" she asked.

Joy bubbled within me. I bounced on my feet, trying not to yell as I replied, "Yes! Yes! That's me! We are good friends and you helped me there!"

"Oh," she yawned and continued, "I don't remember much. All I know is that something happened and I was found unconscious in the game and now I'm here."

"That's okay. We can still be BFFs!" I said, glad that she at least remembered a smidgen.

"Okay," she said, smiling.

My watch beeped and I sighed. What now? But I gasped as I read the message from Agent Barnes.

Meeting room. Now!!!

"I gotta go. See you later!" I said, waving. I dashed out of the room and back up the steps. I ran to the same meeting room where I received my mission. Was there already a new mission? I wasn't in trouble, was I? Wait, maybe I was going to be promoted and receive a star! Whatever it was, being late wasn't going to help.

I ran into the room and grabbed a chair, panting. I looked around. I was the first one here! A second later, Chris came strutting in, but when he saw me, he stopped and lowered his brows.

"How are you—"

"Better luck next time, Chris," I interrupted, giving him a smug smile and forgetting to add his agent title on purpose. I sat down and as the other agents filed in, my stomach filled up with butterflies and I squeezed my eyes shut.

Agent Barnes cleared his throat and my eyes popped open. "Several of you have completed your missions," he started, "and some of you have earned a star."

I wiggled in my chair, trying to get comfortable, and had to suppress an anxious giggle.

"Can you be still for one meeting?" Chris whispered harshly next to me, still upset that I had gotten here before him. I smiled in response.

"Congratulations to…" Agent Barnes announced the few agents who were promoted because of their completed missions. I squeezed my eyes closed again, waiting for my name to be called. "And lastly, Roxie Noble who completed her first mission by catching a thief in Fashion Frenzy."

I jumped out of my seat and let out a whoop. I did it! I'm an agent now! Everyone else in the room stared silently at me and I walked up to the glaring Agent Barnes. I couldn't hold back my grin and his scowl didn't do anything against my mood. I've been working up to this for so long.

"From this day on, Roxie Noble is officially Agent Noble," Agent Barnes finished, giving me a star pin to hook onto my agent suit. I grasped it in my hand, not wanting to lose hold of it even for a second.

After the meeting ended, I raced towards Pops' office and burst through the door.

"Pops! Pops! Guess what?"

He smiled and the wrinkles around his eyes crinkled. "What, dear Roxie?"

"I am now Agent Noble," I said, standing up proudly and putting my fists on my hips.

"Congratulations, Agent!" he said, chuckling. "I knew you could complete your mission successfully."

"There were just a couple of bumps, too!"

"And what did you learn from these bumps?"

I sighed and looked down, toeing the ground with one boot. "I need to have solid proof next time and not assume their actions." I glanced back up.

Pops nodded and smiled. "And remember, we are secret agents as long as the secret stays with us."

I bit my lip and nodded. Even though I always told Pops anything and everything, I couldn't tell him about Rebecca knowing I was a secret agent. She was my friend, so it should be okay...right? I couldn't lose another friend. But if they did find out...I could be terminated. Losing my life as an agent...I shuddered at the thought.

"Well," Pops said, slapping the desk and startling me out of my thoughts. "You should start training again. Who knows when you will get another mission?"

I broke out into a grin and dashed out of his room, fearful thoughts dissipating as hopeful ones prevailed again. I let out a squeal and leaped through the doors of the training room. Agent life was the best life.

Acknowledgments

I would like to thank Mr. Jesse and Mr. George for being my amazing editors. I enjoyed working with y'all and learning from my mistakes. This book wouldn't be the same without your help!

Also, thanks to my family: Mom, Dad, John, Michael, and Ben. You've supported and encouraged me through this fun journey. Thank you for the business advice, coaching, and inspiration!

And finally, thank YOU for reading my story! I hope you enjoyed it as much as I did writing it. Oh my CRABCAKES! You are so amazing and I can't wait to write more about Roxie's adventures for you…which will be soon.

Bye for now! *Air highfive*